That's not my Hobby!

Rosalie Eisenstein

Illustrated by Andy Hammond

RIGBY

In school today, my teacher said,
"Write a letter to a friend telling
them about your hobby."
I do not have a hobby, so I did
not write the letter.

Letter writing

Address
Date

Dear

Yours

"You must find a hobby, Katy,
and you must write the letter,"
said my teacher.
So now I have to find a hobby.

3

Chris has a hobby.
He swims every day.

My ears get blocked up when
I go swimming.
So swimming is not my hobby.

5

"You could play the drums," said Jan.
"Drumming is a good hobby."
Jan taps all the time.

I asked my mum about drums but she said, "NO!" Just, "NO!"
So drumming is not my hobby.

Mrs Jones next door said,
"Why not try knitting?
Knitting is a good hobby.
I will teach you."

I tried knitting but my knitting got smaller, not bigger.
So knitting is not my hobby.

Dad said I could go running with him.
"OK," I said. But his running is not
what I call running.

He took ages to get ready.

Then he stopped to talk to other joggers.

He talked about feet.

He talked about backs.

He talked about feet again.

So running with Dad is not my hobby.

"You could try cooking," said Mum.
I liked cooking. I made a great pie, but
then I had to do the washing up.

"Real cooks have helpers to wash up," I said.

"I'm a real cook," said Mum. "You can be
my helper."

So cooking is not my hobby.

"You could try gardening," said Grandpa.
So I helped Grandpa pull out weeds.

The next day, the weeds were back.
"These are new weeds," said Grandpa.
New weeds or old weeds, gardening is
not my hobby.

17

"Video games are a good hobby," I said.

"No, they're not," said my mum.
"Find a hobby outside."

"You could wash my car," said my brother, Tom.

So I washed Tom's car, well some of it.

Washing cars is not my hobby.

Then I got a letter. It was
from a boy in Canada.
He wanted to be my pen pal.

His letter was cool.

It said:

12, Fir Tree Crescent
Toronto M9W 99X2
CANADA

Tuesday March 15

Dear Katy,
    My teacher asked me to write a letter to a pen pal. He told me to write about my hobby, but I don't have a hobby.
    So, nice to meet you.

Stay cool,
Adam.

Next week, my teacher asked,
"Did you write the letter?"
"Yes, Mrs Riley," I said.

23

I write to my pen pal all the time.
My pen pal writes to me. We write about
all the things we do.
Writing letters is my hobby.